Hubble & Hattie

THE WANDERING WILDEBEEST

Written by
Martin Coleman

Illustrated by
Tim Slater

The Hubble & Hattie imprint was launched in 2009, and is named in memory of two very special Westie sisters owned by Veloce's proprietors. Since the first book, many more have been added, all with the same objective: to be of real benefit to the species they cover; at the same time promoting compassion, understanding and respect between all animals (including human ones!)

Our new range of books for kids will champion the same values and standards that we've always held dear, but to the adults of the future. Children will love reading, or having these beautifully illustrated, carefully crafted publications read to them, absorbing valuable life lessons whilst being highly entertained. We've more great books already in the pipeline so remember to check out our website for details.

Other books from our Hubble & Hattie Kids! imprint

9781787111608

9781787112926

9781787113060

9781787113077

9781787113121

www.hubbleandhattie.com

First published August 2019 by Veloce Publishing Limited, Veloce House, Parkway Farm Business Park, Middle Farm Way, Poundbury, Dorchester, Dorset, DT1 3AR, England. Tel 01305 260068/Fax 01305 250479/email info@hubbleandhattie.com/web www.hubbleandhattie.com ISBN: 978-1-787113-86-2 UPC: 6-36847-01386-8 © Martin Coleman, Tim Slater & Veloce Publishing Ltd 2019. All rights reserved. With the exception of quoting brief passages for the purpose of review, no part of this publication may be recorded, reproduced or transmitted by any means, including photocopying, without the written permission of Veloce Publishing Ltd. Throughout this book logos, model names and designations, etc, have been used for the purposes of identification, illustration and decoration. Such names are the property of the trademark holder as this is not an official publication. Readers with ideas for books about animals, or animal-related topics, are invited to write to the publisher of Veloce Publishing at the above address. British Library Cataloguing in Publication Data – A catalogue record for this book is available from the British Library. Typesetting, design and page make-up all by Veloce Publishing Ltd on Apple Mac. Printed in India by Replika Press.

You may have heard of the
wildebeest,
for weeks, they walk from
west to east

(Or could it be from east to west?
It's hard to know which
way is best)

But they'd require special roofs
(plus, it's hard to brake with hooves)

The reason is the baking sun,
it's way too hot for anyone!
So wildebeest can only think,
"Where can we find a nice cold drink?"

But peering forward and behind,
dry, cracked mud is all they find.
So off they set, towards the ridge
(dreaming of a well-stocked fridge)

The dusty plains are wide and vast,
so wildebeest don't walk too fast.
(They'd get exhausted in the heat,
and nasty blisters on their feet)

Now and then their eye might catch
a small and thorny grassy patch.
But without a proper dinner,
Wildebeest will just get thinner

So, all at once they gallop off
in pursuit of grass to scoff.
But wait! A river, deep and wide,
and buffalo ... the other side!

The leader cries,
"Don't be afraid.
Across the river we
shall wade!"
So down the muddy
bank they slip
to quench their thirst
and take a dip

But then they spot the
sneaky smiles
of underwater crocodiles,
who lie in wait to gorge and
feast
on river-crossing wildebeest!

Lurking there beyond the shore,
fifteen, twenty, maybe more!

It looks impossible to reach
the far-side destination beach!

A buffalo, who's six that day,

excitedly steps up to say ...

"Yoohoo! Hello, all you crocs!

"Look at my new birthday socks!"

This clever, simple footwear mention
grabs every single croc's attention,
and all at once they turn to see
the aforementioned hosiery

Seizing what is now their chance,
the wildebeest all skip and dance

Until at last, they climb the bank!
Then, one by one, they queue to thank

So, for thankful wildebeest,
tummy size has now increased.
But they'll keep wandering, I fear,

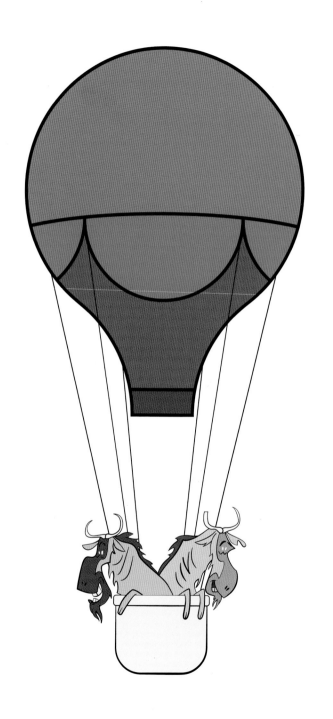